TRICK OR TREAT, BABY SHARK

Doo Doo Doo Doo Doo Doo

Art by John John Bajet

Cartwheel Books
An Imprint of Scholastic Inc.
New York

On a dark spooky night
Deep down in the sea
BABY SHARK and his
Friends wondered,
Who can we be?

Try on these costumes,
It's time to have fun.
We need to get ready,
Halloween has begun!

Let's say BOO, doo doo doo doo doo doo.
Let's say BOO, doo doo doo doo doo doo doo.

Let's say BOO, doo doo doo doo doo doo.

LET'S SAY BOO!

Now let's ROAR, doo doo doo doo doo doo.
Now let's ROAR, doo doo doo doo doo doo doo.

Now let's ROAR, doo doo doo doo doo doo.
NOW LET'S ROAR!

Save the day, doo doo doo doo doo doo.
Save the day, doo doo doo doo doo doo.

Say HEE-HAW, doo doo doo doo doo doo.
Say HEE-HAW, doo doo doo doo doo doo.

Say HI-YAH, doo doo doo doo doo doo.
Say HI-YAH, doo doo doo doo doo doo doo.

Let's rock out, doo doo doo doo doo doo.
Let's rock out, doo doo doo doo doo doo doo.

Let's rock out, doo doo doo doo doo doo.
LET'S ROCK OUT!

Off we go, doo doo doo doo doo doo.
Off we go, doo doo doo doo doo doo doo.

Peek inside, doo doo doo doo doo doo.
Peek inside, doo doo doo doo doo doo.

Peek inside, doo doo doo doo doo doo.

PEEK INSIDE!

Run and hide, doo doo doo doo doo doo.
Run and hide, doo doo doo doo doo doo.

Run and hide, doo doo doo doo doo doo.
RUN AND HIDE!

Trick or treat, doo doo doo doo doo doo.
Trick or treat, doo doo doo doo doo doo.
Trick or treat, doo doo doo doo doo doo.

TRICK OR TREAT!

TRICK OR TREAT,
BABY SHARK!

TRICK OR TREAT, BABY SHARK DANCE!

LET'S SAY BOO!

Cup your hands around your mouth and say, "boo."

NOW LET'S ROAR!

Pretend to be a dinosaur and roar.

SAVE THE DAY!

Strike a superhero pose.

SAY HEE-HAW!

Gallop around and swing your lasso.

SAY HI-YAH!

Do a chop with your hand.

LET'S ROCK OUT!

Play the air guitar.

OFF WE GO!

Skip around the room.

PEEK INSIDE!

Shade your eyes and take a peek.

RUN AND HIDE!

Run like crazy!

TRICK OR TREAT!

Hold out your imaginary trick or treat bag.